MORE
Homer Price

From CENTERBURG TALES

Written and illustrated
By ROBERT McCLOSKEY

SCHOLASTIC BOOK SERVICES

Published by Scholastic Book Services, a division
of Scholastic Magazines, Inc., New York, N. Y.

Copyright 1951 by Robert McCloskey. This edition is published by Scholastic Book Services, a
division of Scholastic Magazines, Inc., by arrangement with The Viking Press, Inc.

3rd printing . . . . December 1966

Printed in the U.S.A.

CONTENTS

Also by Robert McCloskey:

Make Way for Ducklings
*Homer Price
Blueberries for Sal
One Morning in Maine
Time of Wonder

*Available from Scholastic Book Services

I

Experiment 13

THE CENTERBURG COURTHOUSE CLOCK was just striking eight as Homer rode into the town square. He parked his bike in front of the barbershop, poked his finger into a crack in the wooden barberpole, and pulled out a key. After unlocking the door and putting up the shades, Homer swept the floor.

By quarter of nine Homer had finished with all of his opening-up chores. He started looking through the stack of old magazines — the same magazines that had been there last Saturday and the Saturday before, the same magazines that had been in the barbershop since Homer started working there. Homer had looked at them all a hundred times, so he just sat looking out of the window, waiting for the barber to arrive at nine o'clock.

Through the barbershop window he watched the sheriff walk across the square at ten minutes to nine, as usual, and go into Uncle Ulysses' lunchroom for breakfast.

He watched the mayor drive up and go into the town hall at five minutes of nine, as usual.

The courthouse clock struck nine, and Homer yawned. Just for variety he looked in the mirror, so that he could see the town square backwards. Then, by sitting in the barber chair and leaning way back, he looked in the mirror and saw the town square *upside down* and backwards. Homer smiled as he watched the barber come out of the lunchroom upside down.

Boosting himself out of the barber chair, Homer looked at the clock and thought, "He's a little bit late, as usual!" Then he said, "Gosh!" to nobody in particular. "Everything is so *usual* around here. Seems as though nothing ever happens here any more."

"Morning, Homer," the barber said as he came in. "I see we are open and ready for business." It was the same thing that the barber said every Saturday morning.

"Good morning, Mr. Biggs," said Homer, watching the barber take off his coat and hat and hang them on the same hook he always hung them on.

"Now he will put on his eyeshade," thought Homer, "and his white jacket with the two buttons missing. Next he will take his razor from the little white cabinet marked STERILIZER and begin to strop it."

While the barber was stropping his razor the door opened and Homer knew exactly who it would be. He said, "Hello, Sheriff!" without even having to look.

"Good morning, everybody," the sheriff greeted and sat down in the barber chair to be shaved.

Just as the barber finished shaving the sheriff and

Homer finished shining the sheriff's shoes, Uncle Ulysses arrived right on schedule and just as usual.

"Anything new?" asked Uncle Ulysses.

Homer shook his head, and the barber said, "Nope."

"Things are mighty slow," said the sheriff with a yawn.

"No new magazines?" asked Uncle Ulysses hopefully, looking through the same old stack. Then he glanced up and said, "Uh-owh!" and the sheriff, the barber, Homer, and Uncle Ulysses moved over to the window to look.

Dulcy Dooner and Lawyer Stobbs were hurrying across the square just as fast as they could go.

"Something's up!" said the barber.

"Where are they going?" mused Uncle Ulysses.

"Looks like they're beaded for the hank — I mean headed for the bank!" said the sheriff.

"The bank doesn't open until nine thirty," said Homer.

Clear across the square they heard Dulcy bang on the door of the bank and shout, "Open up! Open the door, I say!" And they saw the door of the bank open two minutes before nine thirty, and Dulcy and Lawyer Stobbs go inside.

"First time the bank ever let anybody in before

nine thirty for as long as I remember," said Uncle Ulysses.

"Dulcy is sure excited about something," said the sheriff. "Usually he isn't even up this time of day."

"Say, Homer," said the barber, looking in the cash drawer, "I seem to be running out of change. You take these two dollars and run over to the bank and get me some nickels."

"All right, Mr. Biggs," Homer agreed, and the sheriff and the barber and Uncle Ulysses stood by the open door while he ran across the square and into the bank.

"Sh-h, listen!" said Uncle Ulysses. "I can hear Dulcy shoutin'."

"He just yelled *'ninety grand,'*" whispered the barber.

"No, he didn't," Uncle Ulysses disagreed. "He said *'I demand'.*"

"Here comes Homer," said the sheriff. "We'll soon know what the fuss is all about. What's goin' on, son?" he asked.

"Has Dulcy got ninety grand?" asked the barber reaching for his two dollars' worth of nickels.

"What's he demanding?" asked Uncle Ulysses.

"Dulcy is demanding and *maybe* he's got ninety grand. That's what he's demanding to find out," said

Homer. "Dulcy's uncle Durpee Dooner died of fever over in Africa and he left everything to Dulcy."

"That's nothing to be so mad about," said Uncle Ulysses.

"Naw," the barber agreed, "Dulcy will be a rich man."

"Havin' money should make him easier to get along with," said the sheriff.

"Well, Dulcy hasn't got any money — not yet, anyway," said Homer. "All he's got so far is that old greenhouse and ten acres of land where Durpee Dooner used to run his seed business before he got to be so famous."

"Why, Durpee Dooner must have made lots of money," said the barber.

"Sure!" agreed the sheriff. "Bein' such a samous fientist — I mean famous scientist — and goin' on expeditions all over the world!"

"Well, Dulcy and Lawyer Stobbs can't find any money. They have looked everywhere and gone through all of the papers. There were no bank books, or stocks, or bonds, or anything. All they found was a key to a safe-deposit box, and that must be where all the money is. Dulcy is so mad because they are making him sign a lot of papers before they let him go in the vault and unlock the safe-deposit box."

"It sounds like things have calmed down over there," said Uncle Ulysses, cocking an ear. "I think I'll just walk across and cash a small check."

"I been needin' a new blotter, so I'll just come along," said the sheriff.

The barber went along to get some more change, and Homer ran along behind to take the sheriff his coat. No telling, the sheriff might need his badge.

As they went into the bank, the banker was just opening the heavy door of the vault.

"Just step inside, Mr. Dooner," he said. "Here is the deposit box, number one hundred and thirteen."

"It's about time," growled Dulcy, jabbing his key into the lock.

The sheriff, the barber, Uncle Ulysses, and Homer all crowded up to the counter and peered through the bars to watch.

Dulcy turned the key and pulled out the box. His hands shook so much with excitement that he had trouble opening the lid. He managed to get it open and then let out a wild howl!

"What kinda joke is this?" he yelled, and he jumped around something awful, banging the vault, bumping the banker, and bumping the lawyer.

"Take care, Mr. Dooner! You'll break it!" shouted the banker, grabbing Dulcy by the arm before he could throw the something that was in the box.

"Calm down, Dulcy," the lawyer demanded. "Let's be sensible and take it out in the light and examine it."

"Of all the lousy tricks!" growled Dulcy, holding a small glass jar up to the light.

"What's in it?" Uncle Ulysses demanded through the paying teller window.

"Aw, nuts!" said Dulcy, giving the jar a shake.

"Did you say nuts?" asked the sheriff.

"No!" yelled Dulcy. "It's a lousy jar of *seeds!*"

"A most unusual place for keeping seeds," said the banker.

"Maybe they are unusual seeds," Homer suggested.

"Yes, Dulcy, they are no doubt very valuable seeds," said the lawyer. "That little glass jar might be worth a fortune. Why else would Durpee Dooner keep it locked up in the bank? Look here, there's a label that says EXPERIMENT 13."

The thought of owning a jar of valuable seeds made Dulcy less mad, but he was far from happy. He shook his head sadly and said, "People inherit money every day, and I have to be the one that inherits a jar of seeds — an experiment at that!"

"What are you going to do with your seeds, Dulcy?" asked Homer.

"Well," said Dulcy, rubbing his chin and frowning at the jar, "I'll plant some of them, I guess." He crammed the jar of seeds into his pocket and started for the door.

"Just a minute, Dulcy," the lawyer cautioned "Better keep them locked up here in the bank and take out some of them when you are ready to plant."

"Yes, by all means, Mr. Dooner," advised the banker. "The seeds are apparently very valuable, and you must protect them."

Dulcy thought for a minute, and then did as the lawyer and the banker suggested. He locked the jar of seeds up in the deposit box and went off to his greenhouse to prepare a place to plant.

"Too bad Dulcy didn't find a nice stack of government savings bonds in the deposit box," said Uncle Ulysses when they had arrived back at the barbershop.

"Yup!" said the sheriff. "With savings bonds you know just what's what."

"Dulcy's Uncle Durpee was a great scientist," reminded the barber, "and that jar of seeds might be worth millions."

"Durpee was a great hand at breeding new plants and improving old ones," said Uncle Ulysses. "He was an up-and-coming fellow for his generation — far ahead of his time."

"Remember the giant squash he developed?" asked the barber.

"Yup," said the sheriff, "and remember the Durpee Tremadous Tomentoes — I mean Tremendous Tomatoes?"

"The Strawberry Tree was the best thing, I always thought," said Homer.

"But the Durpee Dooner Honey Onion was the most remarkable plant he ever bred," Uncle Ulysses asserted. "Looked just like any old onion, but tasted like honey. A Honey Onion pie with meringue on top is one of the world's best foods. Durpee Dooner was a genius, no doubt about it!"

"Well, what do you think Dulcy's seeds will grow into?" asked the barber.

"They were little bitsy things like grass seed," said Homer.

"Something rare that old Durpee brought back from one of his expeditions to Asia or Africa, no doubt," said Uncle Ulysses.

"No," said Homer, "the jar was labeled EXPERIMENT

13, so the seeds must be for some sort of plants that he developed himself."

"*Farmer's Almanac* says ·a mild spring," said the sheriff.

"Time to start planting next month," said the barber.

"It'll still be a long time though before we find out what Dulcy's seeds grow into," said the sheriff.

"Dulcy's got a greenhouse," reminded Uncle Ulysses.

"Golly," said Homer, "Dulcy can plant *today!*"

And Dulcy did plant that same day. By eleven o'clock he was back downtown with a truck, buying fertilizer and vitamin plant food. And he was back at the bank again before noon to get some seeds. He carefully counted out twelve seeds, and one more for good measure, into an envelope. Once more he locked up the glass jar in his safe-deposit box and rushed off in the direction of his greenhouse.

By four o'clock, when Homer stopped by the green-house, there was Dulcy inside admiring the thir-teen damp mounds of earth where he had planted his seeds.

"Hello, Mr. Dooner," said Homer.

"Hello, Homer," said Dulcy. "I'm pretty tired, and my back is sore from haulin' fertilizer and from spadin'."

"You need some help," Homer suggested. "School is out next month, and Freddy and I could help out doing hoeing and spraying — that is, if the seeds grow into anything."

"You're hired, Homer, and Freddy too!" said Dulcy. "They'll grow all right," he added confidently. "I put two bushels of vitamin plant food around each seed."

"Whe-e-ew!" whistled Homer. "What kind of plants do you think they will be, Dulcy?"

"I dunno," said Dulcy. "But whatever they are, they'll be the biggest and the best."

Sunday afternoon Homer called Freddy on the phone and said, "Hi, Freddy. Have you heard about Dulcy's seeds?"

"Gosh, yes, Homer! Everybody in Centerburg's heard about Dulcy's seeds," said Freddy. "Everybody's talking about them. The minister even preached about them this morning. *'If that's what you sow, that's what you reap.'*"

"Dulcy's already planted thirteen of them," said Homer.

"Yeah, I know," Freddy said. "And the jar said EXPERIMENT 13. My grandmother says no good can come of that."

"That's just superstition," said Homer. "You're not

superstitious, are you, Freddy? Because Dulcy's going to give us a job watering, weeding, and taking care of the plants when school's out."

"Oh gosh, Homer, that'll be swell. Mebbe they will be Strawberry Trees!"

"Nobody knows," said Homer. "But working for Dulcy we'll find out as soon as anybody. We'll stop at Dulcy's tomorrow after school and see what's happening."

"Okay, Homer," said Freddy. "Good-by."

"Good-by, Freddy," said Homer. "See you tomorrow."

Homer and Freddy stopped at the greenhouse the next day after school; they stopped every day all week, and nothing exciting was going on. The seeds had not come up. Dulcy was getting more and more restless, and complaining about his back. Along about Friday he started complaining about a stiff neck from watching so steadily for the seeds to come up.

On Saturday morning Homer was late getting to the barbershop. He rushed in and shouted, "They're up!"

"What's up, son?" asked the sheriff.

"Dulcy's plants! Dulcy's plants are up — all thirteen of them!" Homer said.

"Let's go look!" said Uncle Ulysses, throwing down his magazine.

And the barber and Homer and Uncle Ulysses went over to the greenhouse with the sheriff, in his car.

"Look!" said Dulcy, proudly displaying the thirteen tender green shoots.

"Healthy-looking plants," said the barber.

"You can almost see them grow!" said Uncle Ulysses.

"You *can* see them grow, if you look closely," said Dulcy, and he started scooping vitamin plant food out of a bag and sprinkling it generously around the plants.

Even with a truckload of vitamin plant food to help out, the plants took weeks to get as high as Homer's head. The tallest one of the plants came just to the bottom of his ear on the day school was out and Homer and Freddy started working at the greenhouse.

They sprinkled the plants with vitamin plant food and sprinkled them with water. They carried bags of fertilizer and listened to Dulcy complain about his back.

"Gosh, Homer, it seems like it takes forever for a plant to grow anything but stems and leaves," Freddy complained. "Why can't these things make a few berries or squashes or something, so we'll know what they are?"

"They have got a lot of stems and leaves," Homer agreed. "Sometimes when I look at them I think they'll be bushes, and other times they remind me of vines."

"They're growing faster now that the weather is warmer," said Freddy. "Look, Homer, this one has grown almost a foot today!"

Sure enough, when Homer stood next to the plant the top reached way above his ear; it was way above his *head*.

The next morning when Homer and Freddy arrived at Dulcy's the tops of the plants were right up touching the glass roof of the greenhouse.

"We have to break out some sections of the roof and give them room to grow," shouted Dulcy.

"Gosh, Dulcy, they're going to be trees!" Freddy exclaimed.

"They're really agrowin' now, son!" said Dulcy with a happy chuckle. "You boys grab a couple of hammers and start knockin' some openings in the roof. You want to be careful," he cautioned, "when you break the glass, that it doesn't hurt the plants."

While Dulcy went off downtown to get another truckload of vitamin plant food, Homer and Freddy climbed around on the roof knocking out openings for the plants to grow through.

Freddy swung his hammer, and a pane of glass went out with a loud crash, and a few small pieces slid tinkle-tinkle down the slant of the roof.

"This is the most fun we've had on this job yet, Freddy," shouted Homer with a laugh.

"Yeah, Homer, but there will be a lot of" — *crash*-tinkle-tinkle — "pieces to pick up," said Freddy as he swung his hammer down.

"That's the sort of job that hurts Dulcy's back," said Homer, stopping to rest. "Holy smoke, Freddy! Look at 'em grow!"

"Wow!" said Freddy, and he dropped his hammer.

The plants were pushing right up through the holes in the glass. It seemed as though they were glad to be out in the warm summer sunshine. Homer peered through the glass and saw a large stalk pushing against the roof. He bashed out a hole, and the plant popped through, spread its leaves, and seemed so grateful that Homer said "You're welcome," without thinking.

By the time Dulcy returned with the vitamin food every single stalk was through the roof, pushing its way into the sunshine, the new green leaves rustling in the summer breeze. Dulcy went right to work, spreading vitamin plant food around the bases of the stalks while Homer and Freddy picked up the glass.

As stories of how Dulcy's plants were growing spread through Centerburg, people began to come out to have a look. Dulcy charged fifty cents admission to the greenhouse and made fifty-nine dollars the first afternoon. By the end of the week, however, business was bad. Not that the plants stopped growing, or that people stopped coming out to look. The plants grew faster than ever — that was the trouble. There was three times as much plant *outside* as there was *inside* the greenhouse. Large crowds gathered on the road every day to watch them grow. Dulcy reduced the price of admission to ten cents, but still not many came inside. He was pretty mad about it, but there was not a thing he could do.

"After all, you can't keep people from lookin' at a forest in the middle of a ten-acre lot," said Uncle Ulysses, and that's just about what Dulcy's plants looked like.

One day the rumor went around that there were

melons eight feet across inside the greenhouse. Business improved, but not for long, because there were no melons — not even little ones. There were no berries or fruit of any kind, no vegetables, not even a suggestion of a blossom.

"They ain't very pretty plants," said the sheriff, who was on hand every day to handle the traffic problem.

"They're pretty enough," said Dulcy, taking offense, "and bigger than anything you will ever grow."

"The plants have a familiar shape," said Homer, "and it seems as though I ought to recognize the leaves."

"Maybe they're potatoes, and under the ground," Freddy suggested.

"If they're potatoes Dulcy," said the sheriff with a chuckle, "you'll have to find a sheam stovel — I mean steam shovel — to dig 'em out."

ADMISSION
50¢

"Just you wait and see!" Dulcy shouted. "These plants will grow the biggest — the biggest — well, the biggest *somethings* ever grown," and he stamped into his greenhouse to spread on more vitamin plant food.

Two whole weeks went by, and Dulcy's plants were producing nothing more remarkable than leaves and stems; but leaves and stems they produced like mad. The plants had become the most important feature of the Centerburg skyline, towering way above the Centerburg Courthouse and the smokestack of the Enders Products Company.

"I don't think they're going to bear anything," the barber said one day at lunch in Uncle Ulysses' lunchroom. "They're using up all their strength putting out shoots and leaves. Dulcy should have pruned them down."

"It'll be a big disappointment to Dulcy," said Uncle Ulysses. "He's worked harder on those plants of his than he has since he put up the street signs out at Enders Heights."

"He can try again next year and keep 'em pruned," said the sheriff, brushing a doughnut crumb from his mustache. "He's got plenty more seeds locked up in the bank."

The door opened and, in no special hurry, Homer

walked in and sat down at the lunchroom counter.

"Hello, Homer," said Uncle Ulysses. "Have a dough-nut, fresh from the machine."

"No, thank you, Uncle Ulysses," Homer replied, and he sat quietly at the counter, watching the automatic doughnut machine make doughnuts.

"You not feeling well?" Uncle Ulysses inquired.

"I'm feeling all right," Homer replied. Then he announced, "I know what Dulcy's plants are."

"You do?" asked Uncle Ulysses, and everyone rushed to the lunchroom window and looked across the square to where Dulcy's plants rose high above the trees and buildings on the far side.

"You can just make out from here," said Homer. "There are thousands and thousands of buds on top."

"They look familiar," said the barber.

"That's what I've thought for weeks," said Homer. "It's the size that fools you. Hold your hand so as to cover the trees and buildings, and pretend for a min-ute that the plants are ordinary size."

Everybody did as Homer suggested; then one of the customers began to giggle, then another, and finally all the people in the lunchroom began to laugh.

"Poor Dulcy!" laughed the barber, holding his sides.

"He'll never get over this," chuckled Uncle Ulysses.

"The town will never stop teasing him. Dulcy's plants are just giant-size *weeds!*"

"Yes, but what kind of weeds?" Homer asked without laughing.

Everybody looked again. This time nobody laughed.

"Jiminy Zeus!" cried Uncle Ulysses.

The barber gulped and said, "I'll have to leave town!"

"So will I!" said another customer.

"Me too, I'm leaving today!" said another.

"Dad gum!" the sheriff said. "Now who'd ever thought them plants was *wagreed!*"

"They're ragweed, all right," said Homer, "and I expect they'll blossom in a few days."

"We'd better get the mayor and go see Dulcy," Uncle Ulysses suggested, and the sober little group from the lunchroom started for the Town Hall. The dentist and several patients came out to see what was going on, and they joined the group. So did the plumber, the jeweler, the printer, and the druggist.

"I have a feeling," said the barber, taking leave of the gathering crowd, "that Dulcy will be in one of his arguing moods. I'm going right home and pack my bag. Just the thought of those things makes me sne-sn-s-*hahuruschooh!* — sneeze."

"An awful lot of folk are troubled with hay fever," said the druggist. "Reminds me I had better order a carload of paper handkerchiefs."

"When all those thousands of buds open up and start filling the air with pollen, this place is going to look like the dust bowl," said the dentist.

Uncle Ulysses and the sheriff went on into the mayor's office, while the others waited outside.

Almost at once the mayor came rushing out of the Town Hall. He shaded his eyes with his hand, looked solemnly up and across the square at Dulcy's thirteen colossal ragweeds silhouetted against the afternoon sky.

Everybody knew the mayor was susceptible to hay fever, so they were not at all surprised when he pulled out his handkerchief, just from force of habit. For a minute it looked as if the mayor might start running; but he tucked away his handkerchief, squared his shoulders, and started walking grimly toward Dulcy's.

The crowd followed along behind.

Dulcy came running out to meet them. "They're budding!" he shouted. "They got thousands and thousands of buds! Howdy, Mayor," he greeted. "I was just about to come see you. I wanted to ask you, would you please send the Fire Department out here so's

I can cut off a few sprigs of buds to exhibit? My ladder is too small to reach to the lowest branches."

The mayor was slightly taken aback by Dulcy's request, and couldn't think of what to say or how to begin.

"I could cut off a few sprigs for you, Mayor," said Dulcy generously, to help the mayor decide. "They'll look mighty nice in a vase in your office when the blossoms come out."

"Dulcy, I — I —" the mayor began and could not continue.

Dulcy Dooner looked around at the solemn faces of the crowd? "What's the matter? This is a big thing for Centerburg! Don't you frown at me, Sheriff, I'm bein' a good citizen. My plants will put this town on the map. I'm doin' a lot for this town, so how about loanin' me the town hook and ladder?"

"Dulcy, I — ah — we —" began the mayor unhappily. "As Mayor of Centerburg, I am sorry to inform you that your plants are *ragweeds*."

Dulcy swallowed hard and craned his neck to look up at his tremendous weeds. In the unhappy silence the gay singing of the birds seemed out of place, and the slight rustle of the giant ragweed leaves suddenly sounded ominous in the summer afternoon.

"Ragweeds? Why, durned if they ain't!" said Dulcy. He seemed disappointed that there would be no fruit or berries to sell, but then he smiled and said, "Well, anyway, I got the biggest dang ragweeds in the world! That'll make Centerburg famous! So look, Mayor, how about the ladder?" he asked.

"See here, Dulcy," said the mayor, "ragweed pollen gives people hay fever!"

Dulcy looked around at the worried faces. "Shucks! Don't you trouble yourselves about me. I'll be all right. I never get hay fever."

"In the interest of public health and pursuit of happiness, for the best interest of the town of Centerburg, I ask you as a good citizen to cut down your ragweeds," said the mayor.

"Cut 'em down?" cried Dulcy. "Cut my ragweeds?" he asked as though he could not believe his ears. "No!" he shouted. "No, I won't cut 'em down." And the citizens watched Dulcy turn on his heel, stamp into his greenhouse, and slam the door.

"Didn't argue much," said the sheriff tartly.

The mayor glanced uneasily up at the thousands of giant ragweed buds swaying innocently in the breeze.

"Sword of Damocles!" Uncle Ulysses exclaimed softly. "In a matter of hours the buds will open, the pollen will — I hate to think of it!"

"Time is important," said the mayor. "We must hold a special town meeting this very evening and decide what to do. Everyone come to the Town Hall at seven-thirty. Until then, I'll be at my desk, and I will welcome any and all suggestions," he added humbly, "of how to deal with this, the greatest and gravest threat our town has ever known."

"Homer," Freddy said on the way back to town, "my grandmother was right — EXPERIMENT 13, thirteen plants."

"Superstitious!" Homer replied. "Let's go along with Uncle Ulysses and see what's going to happen."

Uncle Ulysses, the sheriff, the dentist, the printer, Homer, and Freddy found the barber, suitcase in hand, tucking the key to his shop into the crack in the barber-pole. They persuaded him to wait over and attend the town meeting that evening, so he opened the shop and invited them all in.

"If ordinary ragweed gives some people hay fever,"

the printer reasoned, "then these things will be enough to affect everybody!"

"This town will sneeze itself plumb out of the state of Ohio!" the sheriff declared.

"They're growing just west of town too," the dentist said. "The prevailing winds will blow all the pollen smack down our throats."

"Ulysses, you're a man of ideas," said the barber. "What are we going to do?"

Uncle Ulysses was thinking hard. He paced the floor and said, "We could air-condition the town, but it would cost a lot. Not enough time either. Then again, we might drop dry ice in the clouds from an airplane and make it rain. That would keep down the pollen."

"What clouds?" the barber asked gloomily, looking out at the clear blue sky.

"Dulcy might change his mind," said the printer.

"Not Dulcy," said the sheriff. "We might as well decide to take what's comin' and all go to bed with a big supply of haper pandkerchiefs — I mean perper kerpanchiefs — chaper handkepips — dad gum! You know what I mean — tensing clissues!"

Nobody knew what to do. There was a long line of people waiting to buy tickets at the railroad station. Just like the barber, other businessmen, the plumber, the hardware dealer, the jeweler, even Lawyer Stobbs, were closing their shops and offices and hanging out cards saying:

OUT OF TOWN

REOPENING

SHORTLY AFTER

THE FIRST FROST

But everybody stayed in town to attend the town meeting as a last hope.

Toward seven o'clock Centerburg was a town of gloom. As the sun dropped lower in the sky, groups of residents gathered in the square, and as the sun dropped lower the shadows lengthened. The longest shadow by far was the shadow of Dulcy's thirteen giant ragweeds; and the people watched them extend across and darken the square, and ease slowly up and darken Uncle Ulysses' lunchroom, up and darken the movie theater, and last of all the steeple of the Methodist church.

From one corner of the square there came angry shouts, "Let's chop 'em down! Burn 'em! Spray 'em with weed killer! Spray Dulcy too!"

But the sheriff was right on the job. "Hold on boys!" he shouted. "You can't destroy private property in this town. Let's get on into the meeting and solve this thing regular!" And he headed the disturbers into the Town Hall along with everybody else.

Everybody was there, yes, everybody. Dulcy came too. He walked into the hall at the very last minute, and all eyes were turned to the rear where Dulcy stood with the people who could not find seats.

Seeing that his fellow citizens expected him to say something, Dulcy cleared his throat and said, "I been thinkin'. We could solve this problem the democratic way just as easy as that!" He snapped his fingers, and a murmur of hope sounded through the hall.

"Yeah," said Dulcy, gathering courage, "Centerburg doesn't need no crop o' ragweed!"

At this the murmur grew louder, and someone shouted, "Good boy, Dulcy!"

"This town doesn't need ragweeds," he repeated. Then he took a deep breath and said, "When the Government decides the country doesn't need cotton, the Government pays the farmer to plow it under. When the Government decides there's too many potatoes, the Government pays to have 'em destroyed. Now, I reckon, since Centerburg doesn't need no ragweeds — well, I reckon the town ought to pay me so's they can get rid of 'em. I figger a thousand dollars and expenses, paid in cash, ought to be a fair price."

Another murmur went through the hall. The printer rose from his seat and addressed the mayor. "Mr. Mayor, a thousand dollars seems a big price for a crop of ragweed."

"These are big ragweeds, Your Honor," said Dulcy modestly.

"This sum should be paid by the National Government and not by the town of Centerburg," said Lawyer Stobbs.

At this the county agent jumped to his feet and cried, "I make a motion that the town pay Dulcy. By the time we filled out all the papers and sent them to Washington, it would be too late."

"I second that motion!" the barber spoke up.

Over the whispering of the audience the mayor called for silence and said, "A motion has been made and seconded that the town pay Dulcy Dooner one thousand dollars and expenses in cash for his ragweed plants. Because time is short, and at any hour the plants may break into bloom, we will have an oral vote. All those in favor say 'aye.' "

"Aye!" said everyone.

"Anyone against?" asked the mayor. No one spoke.

"Majority rule," said Dulcy. "It's nice we could solve this problem so democratic like."

Then he made his way to the front of the hall and handed the mayor a paper listing his expenses:

70 bags of vitamin plant food @ $4.00 a bag	$280.00
2 assistants @ $13.00 each	26.00
Rubbing alcohol for lame back	7.13
Total expenses	$313.13

The mayor read this aloud and then said, "Added on to the thousand dollars, the total amount due Mr. Dooner is thirteen hundred and thirteen dollars and thirteen cents."

"Homer," whispered Freddy, "there're those numbers again. That means more trouble —"

"Sh-h, Freddy," said Homer. "Look, the town treasurer and the banker are leaving to get the cash for Dulcy."

When the treasurer returned from the bank he carefully counted out thirteen hundred and thirteen dollars in bills into Dulcy's eager hand, and then just as carefully he counted out the dime and one, two, three pennies.

Dulcy stuffed the money into his pockets, and the mayor announced that after the meeting the Fire Department, and any men who might care to volunteer, would cut down the giant ragweeds and attend to the burning of the trunks and stems and blossoms.

The people applauded and cheered with relief, now that the threat had been dealt with. Life in Centerburg would not come to a sneezing halt, and business could be resumed as usual.

The mayor held up his hand for silence. "Now that we are all assembled, is there anything else that should be brought before the meeting?" he asked.

"Yes," said the town treasurer. "This business has left the town finances pretty low. We ought to discuss how to raise thirteen hundred and thirteen dollars and thirteen cents to make the budget come out right."

"We could have some new taxes!" Dulcy suggested happily. "An extra penny on ice-cream cones, a tax on movies, a penny tax here and there, and nobody'd hardly notice it."

"That's impractical," said the banker. "Think of the bookkeeping trying to keep track of a penny here and there. Borrow the money from the bank, and take ten years to pay it back in easy installments."

"Oh, don't do that," Dulcy cautioned. "The town can't be paying for *this* year's ragweed *next* year. Ya see, I got lots more seed locked up in the bank, and next year I'm countin' on a bumper crop o' giant ragweed — maybe a hundred times as much!"

"Homer," whispered Freddy, "how much is a hundred times thirteen hundred and thirteen dollars and thirteen cents?" And the whisper sounded loud over the troubled silence.

"Seem as if our troubles are never over," the mayor said sadly.

Dulcy Dooner seemed to be the only happy person in the whole population of Centerburg. "Say!" he suggested brightly. "How about a tax on doughnuts, say, twenty-five cents a dozen?"

"No!" shouted Uncle Ulysses. "You can't get away with that, Dulcy Dooner! It's preposterous to think that the doughnut eaters of Centerburg are going to pay for your ragweed growing!"

"No need to get mad, Ulysses," said Dulcy. "Let's do this thing democratic."

Uncle Ulysses called out, "Mr. Mayor, I move we put a tax of twenty-five cents on a dozen ragweed seed!"

"I second that motion," said the printer over Dulcy's shouts of *"No! No!"*

When the mayor called for a vote the "ayes" won, and only one person voted "no."

"Mr. Mayor," said the banker, "I move that this tax

be collected immediately, in cash!"

"I second that motion," said the dentist with a chuckle.

There was plenty of chuckling and laughing throughout the hall now, and everybody gleefully voted "aye." Everybody except Dulcy. He voted "NO – O!"

"Mr. Dooner!" chuckled the mayor, "majority rule, remember? Let's be a good citizen about this!"

"You're steppin' on the minority's toes!" Dulcy shouted, but no one seemed to take notice.

The mayor appointed Uncle Ulysses Ragweed Seed Counter and made him chairman of a committee to count the seeds and collect the tax from Dulcy.

Then at last the meeting was over. The people were in a celebrating mood, the fire bell jangled merrily, and the Fire Department took over the rush job of disposing of Dulcy's plants. Groups of singing people were soon clustered about fires of burning ragweed, and it made a pretty sight, what with spotlights of the fire truck alternating red and white flashes. There was the sound of axes and saws, and then the excited cry of "Timbe-e-er!" followed by the earth-trembling *crash* as a stalk of giant ragweed hit the ground.

"There goes the thirteenth ragweed plant," said Freddy with relief.

"You still worried about numbers, Freddy?" Homer asked. Then he said, "Let's go back to the bank and see how Uncle Ulysses is getting on counting ragweed seeds."

Homer and Freddy peeked through the window of the bank; it was closed up tight, and Uncle Ulysses and his committee were not inside counting seeds. Then they looked in the barbershop; the mayor, the sheriff, the barber, and Lawyer Stobbs were playing rummy, but Uncle Ulysses and his committee were not there. They finally found the seed counters in the lunchroom. Uncle Ulysses was hunched over, squinting through a magnifying glass, counting the tiny giant ragweed seeds. Every time Uncle Ulysses counted twelve, the jeweler put down a mark, and the banker, who excelled at arithmetic, was multiplying the number of marks by twenty-five cents to find out how much the tax of twenty-five cents a dozen on ragweed seeds was mounting up to.

And Dulcy — Dulcy was there, watching like a hawk to see that nobody made mistakes in his counting or marking or multiplying. All four were so intent upon their job that they did not notice when Homer and Freddy arrived.

"Three thousand nine hundred and ninety-nine," said the jeweler.

"One, two, three, four, five, six, seven, eight, nine, ten, eleven, twelve," counted Uncle Ulysses.

"Four thousand dozen," said the jeweler .

"Four thousand dozen times twenty-five cents is one thousand dollars' tax," said the banker, "and we still have several thousand dozen seeds inside the jar to count!"

"Looks like the town of Centerburg is going to

make money on this tax," said the jeweler.

"No, it ain't!" cried Dulcy. "Not from me it ain't!" He counted out a thousand dollars and slammed the money down on the table. "There's your durned thousand, and I'm keeping my expenses!" Then he headed for the door.

"Just a minute, Dulcy!" called Uncle Ulysses. "There are a lot more o' yer seeds to count and tax."

"My seeds, my eye!" shouted Dulcy. "You can shove 'em all in your shoe! I never want to look at another seed!" And he slammed the door of the lunchroom on his way out.

"What are you going to do with the seeds, Uncle Ulysses?" asked Homer.

"Oh hello, boys," Uncle Ulysses said. "You're just the fellows we need here. Homer, Freddy, you finish countin' these things. It's pretty fine work and takes a young, sharp eye. We old fellows are pretty tired, and besides, we better go across to the barbershop and report to the mayor."

Homer and Freddy started counting and the committee went off to make its report.

"Gosh, Homer," Freddy complained, "there's still thousands of seeds here to count, and it will take all night! I don't see why they have to be counted anyway. Dulcy isn't going to pay any more tax on them."

"It's important to count them, though," said Homer. "You know something, Freddy, counting and keeping track of every single one of these seeds is just about the most important job in Centerburg."

"More important than being mayor?" asked Freddy.

"Sure," said Homer, "because if one single seed got lost, it might grow into a giant-size ragweed."

"Just one giant-size ragweed might not make everybody sneeze so bad, Homer," said Freddy.

"Yes it would too," Homer said. "If the pollen from one giant ragweed mixed itself with all the common wild ragweed hereabouts, then the next year there would be hybrid ragweed every place."

"Gosh, Homer, just like hybrid corn. The hybrid ragweeds would be bigger than ever!" said Freddy.

Homer nodded his head gravely. "Just supposing somebody subversive, like an enemy, was to capture these seeds, Freddy, and plant them some night right next to the White House and the Capitol!"

"And the President and the Senators and Representatives all started sneezing with hay fever!"

"Yup," said Homer. "The President couldn't hold press conferences and the Senators couldn't make speeches, and I just guess the Government would come to a stop. Everything would get tangled up and disrupt the country. You see, counting these seeds is super-important!" And he picked up the magnifying glass and started to count giant ragweed seeds.

Over across the town square in the barbershop, Uncle Ulysses and the committee had joined the game of rummy, after they had reported to the mayor.

"It's your turn to draw a card, Ulysses," said the sheriff.

"Queen of seeds," said Uncle Ulysses, turning over a card. "Zeus!" he said. "I keep seein' those things in front o' my eyes. Reminds me, I better call up the lunchroom and see how Homer and Freddy are gettin' along." He picked up the phone and gave the number. "Hello, Homer? How're you makin' out? Still have a lot to count, eh?" Uncle Ulysses listened for a minute and then he said, "We thought we'd just lock 'em up in the bank again. Nobody would ever think of plantin' a crop of ragweeds — except Dulcy, that is. If they knew what they was plantin', they wouldn't." Uncle Ulysses listened again and stopped smiling; then he looked worried. "Homer," he said, trying to control his voice, "you just keep right on countin', and be extra careful not to lose a single seed. Don't you worry, son, we'll talk it over and think of a way to get rid of 'em somehow." Uncle Ulysses hung up the receiver and went back to the rummy game with terror in his eyes and fear in his heart.

"Men," said Uncle Ulysses gravely, "we've got to think hard, or this country will be one big sneeze clear from the Atlantic to the Pacific coast! Why, one single enemy plane could sow those seeds from New York to San Francisco in a couple of hours!"

"What are you raving about, Ulysses?" asked the barber.

"It's the strain of counting all those little seeds that's got him upset, I guess," said the banker.

"I'm not ravin' !" said Uncle Ulysses, glaring wildly at the rummy players. "You men put down your cards and listen to me. We have to think and think fast of a way to get rid of those seeds. If the wrong kind of people were to get hold of 'em, it would mean the ruin of this country!"

"Shucks, Ulysses, we're going to lock 'em up again in the safe-deposit vault, so stop worrying and let's get on with the game!" said the printer.

"Stop being so — so — so complacent," Uncle Ulysses sputtered. "Banks get robbed almost every day, and you know it." Then he looked over his shoulder and leaned way over close and whispered hoarsely. "And the kind of people I mean wouldn't stop at nothing!"

"I'll lock them ragweed seeds in the jail," said the sheriff triumphantly. "That'll stop 'em!"

"Rubbish," said Uncle Ulysses. "As many as twenty people have broken out of your jail, Sheriff, and it's a durned sight easier to break in. Besides, the jail has got mice. Suppose some mouse was to take some of those seeds home to a hole in the ground to feed his family? Then where'd we be? Right back where we were with Dulcy, only this time we might not act in time." Uncle Ulysses was excited now, and he shouted, "Bees and bugs! We'll have to get rid of 'em so they won't find 'em! I tell ya, men, if the pollen from just one of these giant ragweeds gets loose and mixes with our wild ragweeds, we'll have hybrid ragweeds bigger even than the giant ragweeds."

All the men finally realized the seriousness of the situation, and they sat glancing uneasily at one another. The mayor was the first to move; he dashed over to the window and looked across the deserted square at the lunchroom.

"There's no use worrying those two boys about this," he said. "But we had better post a guard outside while they finish their counting. Sheriff," he ordered, "you take your gun and cover the front entrance. And Biggs," he said, handing the barber his keys, "you'll find a revolver in the upper right-hand drawer of my desk. You guard the back entrance. The rest of us will stay here and try to dope out a solution to this problem. In case of trouble, fire a shot into the air and we'll be right over to help out."

The sheriff and the barber went out the door, and the rest of the men drew their chairs up close together for a conference.

"Now then," said the mayor, "let's decide what to do."

Nobody said anything for some minutes. They all sat thinking. Then Uncle Ulysses said, "Well, let's decide."

"I've heard tell that birds sometimes plant seeds in out-of-the-way places," said the banker.

"Yeh, birds and mice and bugs. We have to dispose of them some way so they won't get at them," said Uncle Ulysses.

"The most important thing is to keep these ragweed seeds from falling into the hands of enemy agents," said Lawyer Stobbs. "Sneezing could seriously impair the functioning of the executive and the judicial as well as the legislative branches of our Federal Government."

"What can we do with them? Where can we put them? How can we get rid of them so not one seed can fall into the hands of some enemy agent? Or mouse? Or bird? Or bug?" asked Uncle Ulysses, pacing up and down.

"The bank wouldn't be safe," said the banker.

"It wouldn't be safe to bury the seeds," said the printer.

"If we hid them inside a mattress, the mice would find them," said the mayor.

"I was thinking, if we were to hide them up at the very top of the Courthouse tower it might be a good place, but the —"

"Pigeons!" everybody said at once.

"Of course," said Uncle Ulysses, "if we had the time, we could have a special burglar-bug-bird-and-mouse-proof container made to order, something like the Time Capsule that they buried at the World's Fair. That would take months, and it would be a tremendous responsibility to guard those seeds day and night until then."

"I'm for calling in the FBI right now," said the banker. "There isn't a single place under the earth, on the earth, or a steeple over the earth that's a safe place to hide those seeds."

"The ocean!" shouted Uncle Ulysses. "The Atlantic Ocean! The sheriff could take the seeds to Atlantic City and hire a boat to take him to a nice deep spot. Then he could toss the ragweed seed overboard, and that would be that."

"That's it, Ulysses," said the mayor. "There's a train for the East that goes through here at twelve forty tonight. We'll send the sheriff to Atlantic City to sink those seeds!"

"I've got a metal cashbox with a lock and a nice handle," said the banker. "The sheriff could carry the seeds in that and handcuff it to his wrist, so nobody could steal it on the train."

"And I've got some heavy lead type to put in the box, just to make sure it'll sink," said the printer.

"Fine," said the mayor. "You two fellas get the box and weight it with type; and Lawyer Stobbs, you relieve the sheriff at the front of the lunchroom, so he can go home and pack. Ulysses and myself will call the station and make reservations for the sheriff on the twelve forty."

In shortly less than half an hour, the box was ready and back at the barbershop; and five minutes later the sheriff came in carrying his bag, all packed and ready to go. He pulled out a pair of handcuffs, and one side he fastened to his wrist and the other he snapped through the handle of the box.

"You mustn't forget to unfasten yourself before you toss the box, Sheriff," said the printer with a smile.

"This is no time for joking," said the mayor severely. "Now, Sheriff, you realize how much depends on you. Don't speak to strangers on the train," he cautioned, "and as soon as you get to Atlantic City, hire a boat and go out and sink the seeds."

"You can depend on me, Mayor!" promised the sheriff.

"All right," said the mayor, "let's go over to the lunchroom and pick up the seeds."

The mayor led the way across the town square, followed by Uncle Ulysses, the sheriff, the banker, and the printer. Lawyer Stobbs, gun in hand, met them at the door of the lunchroom.

"Everything all right inside?" Uncle Ulysses asked in a whisper.

"Yes," whispered the lawyer, "I think they're all finished with counting. Sh-h! What's that!" he said, pointing his gun out into the shadows of the square.

After a tense moment of waiting, the postmaster's

dog came up, wagging his tail. Everybody relaxed and Uncle Ulysses chuckled, "That dog can smell doughnuts cookin' a mile away! Come on. Let's go inside and pack up the seeds and get something to eat. I'm hungry." He opened the door and went in, followed by all the men and the postmaster's dog.

"Hello, boys. All through counting, I see," said the mayor.

"Ah-h!" exclaimed Uncle Ulysses. "Very thoughtful of you, Homer, to make some doughnuts. The sheriff can take some with him for a snack on the train, and we're all pretty hungry right this minute." He paused to admire his automatic doughnut machine make doughnuts. And as he watched, the machine stopped.

Uncle Ulysses, who had started passing out the hot doughnuts, said, "You didn't mix up enough batter. You should have made more."

"But, Uncle Ulysses, we only meant to make a dozen," said Homer.

"Yeah," said Freddy, who had been counting the doughnuts as they came out of the machine. "We only meant to make a dozen." Then he added miserably, "But it turned out to be thirteen!"

"Well, there's enough to go around, so help yourselves, everybody," Uncle Ulysses offered.

"But Uncle Ulysses —" said Homer.

"Freddy, you go to the back door and call the barber," Uncle Ulysses said, suddenly remembering that the barber was still guarding the rear.

"Uncle Ulysses —" Homer started to say.

"Let's get the seeds in the box and locked up," said the mayor, taking a bite of doughnut, "and then I'd like a cup of coffee."

Freddy came back with the barber, and Uncle Ulysses handed him a doughnut. Then he turned to Homer. "Get the ragweed seeds, son, and put them in that box the sheriff's got danglin' from his wrist."

"But, Uncle Ulysses," said Homer, "that's what I've been trying to tell you!" Then he asked, "Have you ever heard of a berry growing into a berry bush after it had been cooked into a pie?"

Uncle Ulysses had his mouth full of doughnut, and so did all the other men, so they all shook their heads "No."

"Have you ever heard of a nut growing into a nut tree after being baked into a cookie?" Homer asked.

And again all the men nodded their heads, because they were chewing doughnut and trying to swallow.

"Popcorn won't grow after it's been popped either,"

said Freddy. "I know, because I tried it once."

Uncle Ulysses gulped and said, "Homer, you're a good boy, it's gettin' late, and you and Freddy run along now."

After Homer and Freddy had gone, the mayor fed the rest of his doughnut to the postmaster's dog. So did Uncle Ulysses and the barber and the jeweler, the printer, the banker, the sheriff, and Lawyer Stobbs. Then they fed him the rest of the doughnuts and watched silently while he ate up every last crumb. As the last crumb disappeared, the sheriff said "There goes my trip to Atlantic City."

And the barber said, "From now on, every time I look at that dog or even mail a letter, I'll probably have to sn-sn s-s-ss*harahchoowh!*"

Ever So Much More So

THE EARLY-AFTERNOON SPRING SUNSHINE came peeping into the lunchroom and reflected off the stainless steel trim of Uncle Ulysses' unpredictable automatic doughnut machine.

The sun reflected off the shiny metal and right into the eyes of Uncle Ulysses, who was settled comfortably at the counter, having an after-lunch chat with the sheriff and the judge.

Uncle Ulysses blinked his eyes and thought, "I'll have to get up and go all the way outside to wind that awning down. Ought to put a motor on it," he thought, "with a button under the counter, to save all those steps and all the winding." Then he yawned out loud and shifted his position just enough to allow the reflection to go over his shoulder.

"Put a button on it," he said, thinking out loud, much to the confusion of the judge and the sheriff.

"Put what?" asked Homer, who was wiping crumbs off the counter.

"Oh yes, Homer," said Uncle Ulysses with a start. "Put the awning down, like a good fellow, would you please?"

"Okay, Uncle Ulysses," said Homer and, after wiping a pile of crumbs off the counter into his apron, he hustled outside and shook them onto the curb. He watched while the Centerburg Town Hall pigeons started arriving to eat crumbs, then hustled back across the walk and wound down the awning.

"Thank you, Homer," said Uncle Ulysses as Homer came back into the lunchroom.

"Everything look feacepul — I mean peaceful — and law-abidin' out on the square?" the sheriff demanded of Homer.

"Dulcy Dooner is headed in this direction," Homer said.

"Ah-h!" said the judge. "*That* exceedingly uncooperative citizen of our community!"

They all turned and watched through the window of the lunchroom while Dulcy paused next to the monument. The sheriff bristled when Dulcy struck a match on the bronze tablet, casually lit his pipe, and flipped the burned match in the general direction of the statue of "Peace." Then he came on toward the lunchroom, detouring slightly in order to scuffle through the crumbs and frighten a few pigeons.

Slam! went the door of the lunchroom as Dulcy came in. But the sheriff, the judge, Uncle Ulysses, and Homer hardly jumped. They all knew how Dulcy closed doors.

"What are you up to these days, Dulcy?" asked

the sheriff, eying Dulcy carefully as though expecting to find something like packages of strange seeds or bottles of elixir sticking out of his pockets.

"Always suspectin' me!" complained Dulcy. "Sheriff, you're the most suspicious guy in the state of Ohio!"

"In view of several unfortunate occurrences attributable directly to certain actions of one Dulcy Dooner, I am of the opinion," the judge proclaimed in his usual pompous way, "that the suspicions of our sheriff are entirely justified."

"Good afternoon, my friends!" said a strange voice, and the judge, the sheriff, Uncle Ulysses, Dulcy Dooner, and Homer turned to see a stranger walk in the door. He had a case under one arm and a folding stand under the other.

"Good afternoon, my friends," he repeated. "You are without doubt the most fortunate people in the world, and in just one minute — yes, one short sixty seconds of your valuable time — I am going to make you even more fortunate . . . thankful that I have come to you with this sensational introductory offer!"

The stranger, after introducing himself as Professor Ear, "Professor Atmos *P. H.* Ear," talked on and on, scarcely stopping to take a breath, and at the same time managed to shut the door, tip his hat, unfold his stand, set up his case carefully, and take off his gloves, smiling sweetly all the while.

"I have in here," he continued, tapping the lid of his case, "one of the wonders of the world! Yes, my friends — and you *are* my very good friends – in just one minute I am going to reveal to you a product and make you an offer that will change your life, *if* you are the kind of people that get a *bang* out of life," he exclaimed, emphasizing the *bang* with a flourish and swat of his gloves on top of his case. "You are the ones, yes, the very people, that will have the good sense, the intelligence, imagination, ability, good judgment, and love of the finer things in life to apply this amazing product to obtain the beneficial blessings, the sense of well being, and complete, yes, complete, satisfaction that this remarkable product has the ability to impart to each and every one."

"We don't want any o' — " Dulcy started to interrupt.

"*It is my honor,*" continued the professor, loud enough to be heard above Dulcy's interruption, "to bring to you this fabulously amazing and most phenomenal product, and its name is" — he paused dramatically, snapping free the fastenings of the case and throwing up the cover — "its name is EVERSOMUCH MORE-SO!"

The judge, the sheriff, Uncle Ulysses, Dulcy, and Homer all stared at the cans displayed so suddenly before their eyes.

"What —?" Uncle Ulysses started to ask.

"Ah-h, *what?*" echoed the stranger. "Ah-h, yes, my good friends, I can see the question in your friendly faces. *What* is this remarkable EVERSOMUCH MORE-SO, and *what* can this phenomenal EVERSOMUCH MORE-SO do for *me?* In just one minute, just thirty short seconds, I am going to demonstrate to you and prove to you without the shadow of a doubt that this product can accomplish wondrous things.

"Each and every can," said the professor, picking up a can and continuing without a pause, "yes, *each* and *every* can comes complete with a handy adjustable top. A slight twist to either left or right opens the tiny holes in the cap, making EVERSOMUCH MORE-SO readily accessible for instantaneous application.

"Now for the purposes of our demonstration," the professor continued quickly, "we shall use these delicious-looking doughnuts. Young man," he said to Homer, "if you will be so kind as to pass the tray, and if you gentlemen," he requested, bowing low, "would be so kind as to take two doughnuts . . ."

While Homer passed the tray and everyone took

two doughnuts, one in each hand, the professor said, "Now my friends, we are ready to — uht, uht, sonny, don't forget me!" And before Homer could pass the tray the professor speared two doughnuts on the end of his cane.

The judge and Uncle Ulysses exchanged looks, and the sheriff was about to ask, "When —?"

"*Now*," said the professor loudly, banging on his cane for undivided attention, "now we are ready to proceed with our demonstration. Yes, in just one minute — only sixty seconds — but first," said the professor, picking up a can of EVERSOMUCH MORE-SO, "I shall acquaint you with this wondrous product."

The judge, the sheriff, Uncle Ulysses, Homer, and Dulcy all leaned closer, each with both eyes watching the professor twist the adjustable can top, and each with doughnuts in both hands.

"As I proceed, young man," the professor said to Homer, "please pour cups of your delicious coffee for everyone here."

"Ahuumph!" the judge cleared his throat restlessly.

"A cup of coffee costs —" Uncle Ulysses began.

"Everybody eat the doughnut in his right hand!" the professor commanded loudly. "Delicious—uhm-m? Simply delicious," he declared, taking a dainty bite

from the one on the tip of his cane. Having safely stopped all interruptions with large bites of doughnut, the professor continued in a low, confiding voice, "EVERSOMUCH MORE-SO is a truly remarkable product."

He shook some on his doughnut and swung it in front of the noses of his audience, on the tip of his cane, for all to see. "Remarkable, you say!" interpreted the professor, loudly enough to be heard over sounds coming from behind mouthfuls of doughnut. "Yes, my friends, EVERSOMUCH MORE-SO is *invisible!* And what's more, EVERSOMUCH MORE-SO cannot be smelled," he said, passing the can quickly beneath every nose. "You cannot feel it, and you cannot see it," he added, rubbing his fingertips and then wiggling the can close to his ear.

"Pass the coffee, young man!" he commanded Homer and quickly continued his speech. "EVERSO-MUCH MORE-SO is *absolutely invisible* to the naked eye, odorless to the human nose, soundless to the — young man, don't forget the cream and sugar — as I was saying, soundless to the unassisted perceptibilities of the human ear, undetected, by itself, by the sensitive human nerves of touch, and what is more, EVERSO-MUCH MORE-SO, taken from the can in its natural un-adulterated state, is completely tasteless to the sensitive taste buds of the human tongue.

"Now you are about to ask," the professor said, "why should we be interested in this product we cannot see, smell, taste, hear, or feel? But *watch closely!* Sprinkle a small amount of EVERSOMUCH MORE-So in your good aromatic cup of coffee — so! *Immediately,* yes, my friends *im-me-e- ediately,* that good aromatic cup of coffee becomes *ever so much more so!* Yes, indeed, and after sprinkling a few drops of this remarkable, invisible, tasteless, odorless, textureless, absolutely soundless product on the delicious doughnut you hold in your hand, that delicious doughnut becomes immediately *ever so much more so* delicious!"

The can was passed to Dulcy and on to the judge, from the judge to the sheriff, on to Uncle Ulysses, and last of all to Homer. Everyone shook out a small amount of EVERSOMUCH MORE-So into his cup of coffee and onto his second doughnut.

Everybody began tasting carefully, exchanging glances, tasting once more, and nodding solemnly, while the professor talked on and on.

"Yes, my friends, that is indeed the most *ever so much more so* delicious doughnut and the best, yes, without doubt, the most *ever so much more so* aromatic cup of coffee you have ever tasted."

Everyone was nodding in agreement and enjoying his doughnut and coffee — everybody but Homer, who was tasting his coffee and making miserable faces. Finally he asked, "What if you don't like coffee? Does —?"

"Does EVERSOMUCH MORE-SO work on *everything*, this young man wants to know?" the professor said quickly. "Ah, but yes!" he shouted "*Everything*. It will make a rose smell ever so much more lovely, curly hair ever so much more curly, beautiful music ever so much more beautiful. Yes, my friends, surely you are all intelligent enough to realize the far-reaching possibilities of EVERSOMUCH MORE-SO! It comes to you in this convenient can, put up under the most sanitary conditions by the famous Doctor Forscyth Eversomuch in his great open-air laboratory. One can — yes, one single can — lasts a lifetime. After purchasing one can of EVERSOMUCH MORE-SO, a man can rest assured that he will never again want for another can of EVERSOMUCH MORE-SO. It will keep just as fresh, just as free from impurities, just as potent inside the can as the day it was packed. And now for the amazing price of fifty cents — only four bits, one half of one dollar — a lifetime can of EVERSOMUCH MORE-SO is yours. This is one of the good things of the earth, men.

Now don't miss this golden opportunity to own a convenient can of it for this amazing price of fifty cents."

The sheriff counted out fifty cents, the judge bought a can, so did Uncle Ulysses. Even Dulcy borrowed half a dollar from the judge and bought a can.

As the professor prepared to snap shut his case, Homer asked, "If you don't like coffee and you put EVERSOMUCH MORE-SO in it, then will you not like coffee *ever so much more so?*"

"How would you like," the professor asked, "a nice fast kick — eherump — would you like a nice free can of EVERSOMUCH MORE-SO?" And he quickly tossed a can to Homer, snapped up his case, hooked his cane over his arm, pulled on his gloves, tipped his hat, and was out of the door and away in an instant.

"G'by," said Dulcy abruptly. "I'm gonna try this stuff on something."

"Me too," said the sheriff.

"Good day, Ulysses," said the judge, remembering to be polite.

"Um-m," answered Uncle Ulysses absent-mindedly, for he was carefully selecting two doughnuts.

When he and Homer were alone, Uncle Ulysses put the two doughnuts on two plates. One he left plain and the other he sprinkled liberally with EVERSOMUCH

MORE-SO. Then he tasted, first one, then the other — the one with, the other without. He stroked his chin, then called Homer, and they both tasted.

"I'll be durned," said Uncle Ulysses finally.

"You know, Uncle Ulysses," Homer said, "nobody paid for coffee and doughnuts this afternoon."

"I'll be durned," Uncle Ulysses repeated. *"Ever so much more so!"*

The following Thursday Uncle Ulysses sat slumped on his stool behind the counter when the judge walked in.

"Judge," Uncle Ulysses asked sleepily, "do you notice anything different about me?"

The judge looked Uncle Ulysses over carefully and said, "I notice a marked tendency toward sleepiness."

"Uh-uh-uh," nodded Uncle Ulysses with a yawn, "that's what Aggie says. Says I'm lazier than ever — *ever so much more so,* she says. That's not so, Judge. But I just can't seem to sleep at night any more. I put some EVERSOMUCH MORE-SO on my innerspring mattress to make it softer."

"And did it?" asked the judge.

"Yes," nodded Uncle Ulysses, "but I spilled some of the stuff on one of the springs that had a slight squeak, and it seemed to start squeaking *ever so much more so.*

Can't sleep a wink in that bed. Hello, Sheriff," he added as the sheriff came in, looking flustered and red in the face.

"Gentlemen," the judge said solemnly, "I fear that some grave metamorphosis of cerebral or of physical characteristics has erupted within my innermost self. In fact," he said pompously, "I am just exactly like myself, only *ever so much more so.*"

"Tomesimes," said the sheriff sadly, "I wix my mords all up, but sis thuff ixxes 'em mup so I don't even snow what I'm krying to snay!"

"I think," said Uncle Ulysses gravely, "that we are imaginin' the whole thing. A man just *can't* be more like himself than he is already. Let's ask Dulcy," suggested Uncle Ulysses.

And indeed there was Dulcy, stamping across the grass in the square. He stumbled over a KEEP OFF THE GRASS sign, let out a loud bellow, picked up the sign and threw it in the general direction of "Peace." "Peace" went kabonk! as the sign smacked into her. After knocking over a trash can, Dulcy came on toward the lunchroom.

"He's *ever so much more so,* all right. Been eatin' it every day, I bet," said Uncle Ulysses while the sheriff and judge nodded.

Slam! went the door as Dulcy came in. Homer and Freddy came in soon after and looked concernedly at ever so drowsy Uncle Ulysses, at the ever so pompous judge, the ever so flustered and suspicious sheriff, and the *ever so much more so* uncooperative citizen named Dulcy Dooner.

"How *you* feelin', Homer?" Uncle Ulysses asked.

"Just fine, Uncle Ulysses," Homer answered. "You look sleepy, Uncle Ulysses. Got spring fever?"

"What did you do with your can of EVERSOMUCH MORE-SO, Homer?" asked Uncle Ulysses, trying to keep awake and unconcerned.

"Oh, *that* stuff," said Homer. "Freddy and I put a lot of it on my radio to improve the reception. It seemed a little better, but it seemed to make ever so much more static and interference too. So we took a screw driver and pried the top off the EVERSOMUCH MORE-SO can, just to see what was inside."

"Yes?" everybody asked.

"Yes," said Homer.

"It was empty," Freddy said with a shrug.

"That stuff is invisible," Dulcy reminded.

"Well, it was an empty can!" said Freddy defiantly.

"And what could be more empty than an EVERSOMUCH MORE-SO empty can?" asked Homer.

"We've been dindled, doggonit — I mean swindled," howled the sheriff.

"Our fertile imaginations have led us astray," pronounced the judge.

"The professor took us, all right," chuckled Uncle Ulysses, seeming to come more awake of a sudden.

"Here, Judge," said Dulcy, handing over his can of EVERSOMUCH MORE-SO. "Now we're even and I don't owe you fifty cents."

"Help yourselves to doughnuts, boys," Uncle Ulysses said solicitiously, the way he always did before asking a favor.

"Boys," he said, "we can't let this affair come to the attention of Grampa Hercules, or we'll never hear the end of it."

Homer hesitated until both he and Freddy had helped themselves to doughnuts and then said, "He already knows."

"What?" cried the sheriff and Uncle Ulysses.

"Yep. I put the top back on the can and decided to give it to Grampa Herc. It's the sort of thing he would appreciate ever so much, you know," Homer said.

"And what did the gold oat — I mean, what did the *old goat* say?" demanded the sheriff.

"He said it beat all what the world was coming to, didn't he, Freddy? And he said," Homer continued, "that it used to come in bulk when he was young, and lots cheaper too. Nobody bothered to give it a fancy name or put it in a package with an adjustable top."

"Continue, young man," the judge suggested.

"Well," Homer said, "he allowed as how he'd never tried this *packaged* kind of Eversomuch More-So, and he had a feeling he'd like to see if it was just as strong as the old-fashioned kind. So I sold him *my* can for a dollar."

"That's my nephew, and more so," said Uncle Ulysses.

"We been swindled!" repeated the sheriff. "I shoulda locked that fella up!"

"*Entirely* outside the law!" the judge proclaimed.

"Helloooo, everybody!" said Grampa Hercules, letting himself in the door.

Uncle Ulysses sighed and wondered to himself how more so Grampa Herc could possibly get.

"How do you feel, Hercules?" the judge inquired.

"Never felt so good in my whole life!" answered Grampa Herc.

"Okay, what did you do with it?" demanded Dulcy.

Grampa Herc looked puzzled; then he said, "Oh,

you mean the stuff in the can, the EVERSOMUCH MORE-So. Wu-a-ll, you know, I got to thinkin'. An old fella like me ain't got long to spend in these parts. I can use up a lot o' time sprinklin' a bit on this and that, here and there. I thought to myself, what's one big, all-fired-honest-to-crawfish, powerful, important way to use up a lifetime supply of EVERSOMUCH MORE-So? I thought and I thought, and finally it come to me. I went out in my backyard and hunted up a nice soft spot of black earth. Then I started to shake that stuff on that wonderful earth as hard as my arm could shake. I shook until my arm got tired, and I reckon the can was just about empty. Then I took a screw driver and pried off the lid and poured the EVERSOMUCH MORE-So can full of water, and *do you know,* that was the *dampest,* the *soakenest,* wringin' wettest sloppin'-to-goodness can of water I ever laid eyes on!"

"Yes?" said Uncle Ulysses.

"Yep!" said Grampa Herc. "And then I dumped that EVERSOMUCH MORE-So soakingest water onto that good old earth and watched it soak in, right down to the core — somewhere halfway between here and China. Then I looked around me and noticed how green the grass looked — trees budding, birds singing, and I felt good all over! See, look out there in the square — just like I'm tellin' you. It's a great old world!" shouted Grampa Herc, leaping up and clicking his heels, "and what's more, it's getting better all the time! So long everybody!"

Uncle Ulysses, the sheriff, the judge, Dulcy, Homer, and Freddy all walked out into the square in the nice warm spring sunshine.

"Do you think I ought to give this fifty cents back to Grampa Herc?" asked Homer, holding out half a dollar.

"You just loan that to me, Homer," said Dulcy, making a grab, "and I'll buy my can back from the judge. You can owe Grampa Hercules the *other* fifty cents."

"Homer," said Uncle Ulysses, "run back to the lunch-room and bring a screw driver from the tool box. Freddy, you go along and bring a pitcher of water."

Uncle Ulysses was scraping up a nice soft absorbent spot under an old maple right near the statue of "Peace."

"You know," he said, "it's really a waste of time to shake it on. We'll just fill it right up to the top and let it keep arunnin' over and soakin' in!"

3

Pie and Punch
and You-Know-Whats

U NCLE ULYSSES stood near the door of his lunchroom, leaning on his new automatic jukebox.
While he peered out across the square toward the
lighted windows of the Centerburg Public Library,
his face gradually changed from pink to a deep beet-
red. It turned lavender for a fleeting moment, then
faded off into a flickering grassy-green color. Uncle
Ulysses was not feeling sick, but he'd been changing
colors like this for several days now — ever since he'd
acquired his beautiful new automatic jukebox. The
new jukebox had brilliant lights inside that automatically changed color every few seconds, and anybody or
anything that came within ten feet of the jukebox
automatically changed color too.

No, Uncle Ulysses was not feeling sick, but he was
feeling impatient; and just as he — and the jukebox —
automatically turned lavender for the seventeenth
time, the door opened, and in walked Homer and
Freddy.

"Hi, Uncle Ulysses!" Homer greeted. "Sorry we're
late. We picked out a lot of books this evening, because the library's going to be closed for two weeks."

"The librarian is going away on a vacation," Freddy
explained, "so we picked out enough books to last until
she comes back."

"I heard that she was going to Yellowstone Park with the sixth-grade teacher," said Uncle Ulysses, who kept pretty close track of things like that.

"Yep," said Homer, "and she promised to send us a postcard with a picture of Old Faithful on it."

"That'll be nice," said Uncle Ulysses, listening politely. Then he said, "Boys, I'm goin' over to the barbershop for a spell, so you two fellows help yourself to doughnuts and look after things while I'm gone."

"Okay, Uncle Ulysses," Homer said, and then he watched patiently while Uncle Ulysses went from one of his automatic gadgets to the next — first turning them on and then turning them off, just to make sure they would stop. It was a slight nervous habit that Uncle Ulysses had developed of late, and it seemed to be more noticeable right before he planned to leave Homer in charge of the lunchroom. He checked them off one by one — waffle irons, toaster, doughnut machine, dishwasher. Last of all, he walked over to check his new automatic jukebox. He gave it an affectionate pat (it was a pink pat, because the automatic lights happened to be pink at the moment). He punched a button to select a number called "Boogie Woogie Symphony," and dropped a nickel (a green one) into the green slot of the jukebox. There was a *cl-l-lick!*

and mysteriously and silently the record that Uncle Ulysses had selected slid out of a large stack and began to spin.

"Golly," said Freddy, "it seems almost like magic!"

Uncle Ulysses smiled orangely, and they all three stood entranced, listening to the beautiful full-bodied tones of a boogie-woogie symphony orchestra.

"It almost seems to hypmatize you!" Homer exclaimed as he listened to the music and watched the record spin and the lights shift slowly from one color to another.

Uncle Ulysses nodded proudly, and as the music ended on an odd minor boogie-woogie note, he watched tensely while some mysterious automatic fingers inside the jukebox silently slipped the record back into the stack.

"There," he said, visibly relieved, "that *works* perfectly, and it *stops* perfectly! Here are a couple of nickels, boys, you can have some music while I'm gone."

Homer and Freddy thanked Uncle Ulysses, and after he had gone off to the barbershop they sat silently for some moments, watching the colored lights inside the jukebox slowly change from one color to another.

"Hawh!" Freddy looked at Homer and smiled weak-

ly. "You sure look funny, sitting over there in that green light!"

"Hawh yourself," Homer answered. "You don't look so hot either, especially when you're turning blue all over! C'mon Freddy, have a doughnut, and let's look at our library books."

Homer and Freddy had finished their doughnuts and were trying to decide which books to read first and which to save until last when a stranger opened the door and stalked into the lunchroom.

"Good evening," he said softly, brandishing a flat parcel and turning slowly from rosy pink to deep purple, along with the parcel and the lights in the jukebox.

"I have brought a recording to put in your jukebox," he said, furiously fumbling with the strings and paper of his parcel. "It will be number one on the *bit* —" The stranger broke off suddenly and stood quietly in order to change colors and to compose himself.

Homer and Freddy changed colors, too, while they watched and waited silently.

Then the stranger, having calmed down to some extent, repeated, "It will be number one on the *Hit Parade!*" He finished undoing his package and produced a recording, which he carelessly tossed almost to the ceiling. Then he stood motionless, his arms dangling limp at his sides, watching it drop. The record landed with a *crash!* on the lunchroom floor. Homer and Freddy gasped, and the stranger laughed.

"Unbreakable!" he said, chuckling. He picked up the record and bent it almost double. "Absolutely, disgustingly unbreakable! I've *tried* to break it — goodness knows I've *tried*," he said as though he were apologizing to Homer and Freddy. He then turned purposefully and unlocked the glass front of the jukebox. "I'll put it right here between 'Boogie Woogie Symphony' and 'Boogie Woogie Polka,'" he said, sliding the record into the stack. Then he quickly snapped the glass case shut and locked it with a flourish.

"There!" he said with great relief and a slight change of hue, "that's that!"

The two boys felt relieved, too. They had gotten over being startled by the sudden appearance of this odd stranger. Homer, remembering his job, put down the book he had been holding and went behind the counter.

"Would you care for a snack to eat, sir? A sandwich and a cup of coffee?" he asked. "Some nice fresh doughn —"

"Uht! Uht! Uht! Uht!" the stranger interrupted, wagging his finger violently, before Homer could finish saying "doughnuts."

"I *never, never* eat them," he confided. Then, leaning way over, he whispered, "They're positively full of *holes*, you know! They're simply full of *whole holes!*"

Homer thought about that for a moment and then shrugged his shoulders. "How about a piece of pie, sir?" he asked pleasantly.

"Oh me, oh my!" the stranger gasped. "I *never, never* eat *hip!*" He hiccupped. "I never eat *hip* pie, because the very thought of *hip* pie makes me *hip* hiccup!"

Homer quickly filled a glass with water and handed it to the stranger. "Hold your breath and count to ten while you drink this!" he commanded. And the stranger meekly did as he was told. "That always cures my hiccups," Homer explained.

"It cures my hiccups too," said Freddy, "but I don't get 'em from thinking about p —"

"Uht! Uht! Uht!" sputtered the stranger, waving an arm wildly and almost dropping the glass. He looked reproachfully at Freddy and then turned to Homer. "Thank you, young man, for curing my hiccups. I must go now; I really must be going," he said, turning toward the door. He appeared anxious to be gone before something dreadful could happen.

"Hey, mister," Freddy called, "you forgot to put a name for the new record here next to the selector buttons!"

"Oh," said the stranger, pausing with his hand on the door, "it hasn't any name. It's — ah — just one of those things. And by the way," he added *"don't play it!* I beg of you to never set needle to its black unbreakable surface, and *never* let its sounds escape from this beautiful, gaudy jukebox." The stranger paused while Homer and Freddy nodded and gulped.

Suddenly, without the least trace of humor, the stranger laughed, "Hah, hah, hah!" and changed to a lovely shade of blue-green. "*But you will*," he whispered, taking on an amethyst tinge. "Now, good night, my proud, parturient pair of panted Pandoras!"

Then the door closed ever so grass-green and softly.

"That character," said Freddy after a long silence, "could make some little squirrel very happy. What did he mean, Homer, when he called us a 'proud parturient pair of panted Pandoras'? A Pandora is an animal, isn't it? Why did that screwball call us a couple of proud animals with pants on?"

"You're thinking of panda, Freddy," said Homer. "But *Pandora* is a girl's name."

"He called us *girls!*" cried Freddy, doubling his fists in frustration. "Now how's that for a character! He calls you a girl with words that are over your word level!"

"He didn't exactly call us girls, Freddy," Homer said thoughtfully. "At least not just *any* old kind of girl. Pandora was somebody famous — like Pocahontas or Molly Pitcher. Seems as though I've read something about her doing something very special, but I can't remember what. We have to find out exactly what this dame Pandora did before we'll know exactly what he meant. It might be a sort of a clue, Freddy. And that word 'parturient' — mebbe we ought to find out what *that* means. I'll match you, Freddy, to see who runs over to the library to look 'em up," Homer suggested, producing a nickel from a pocket of his blue jeans and giving it an expert flip.

"Okay," Freddy agreed, producing his nickel and flipping too.

"They're both heads," said Homer when they had uncovered their coins, "so you have to look 'em up, Freddy."

"Well, all right, if you think it's absolutely necessary, Homer, but I still think the guy was nuts. I'll look up 'parturient' in the dictionary, but where will I look to find out about that Pandora dame?"

"She might be in the dictionary, too," Homer said, "but if she isn't there, you'll have to ask the librarian where to find her."

"All that trouble to find out about some silly dame!" said Freddy disgustedly. Then he grumbled something about screwballs in general and went scuffling out of the door, muttering, " 'Proud, parturient pair of panted Pandoras!' Cripes! The guy musta had 'P's' for supper!"

"Did you get the dope, Freddy?" Homer asked expectantly when Freddy came scuffling back into the lunchroom.

"Yeah," said Freddy, assuming the look of a martyr because of all the mental effort he had just put forth. "She was a dame, and she had a box that she wasn't supposed to open the lid of or let anything out of. And she did. And what came out was a lot of some kind of trouble things that must be extinct by now, because the whole thing happened such a long time ago. And 'parturient,'" Freddy continued, "means 'just about to let something out.' So you see, Homer, first he tells us not to, then he tells us we will, then he tells us we shouldn't, and then the screwball says we're 'parturient' and just about to! The guy was nuts, Homer. I'll flip you to see who plays the record first."

"Well," said Homer doubtfully, "mebbe we better not — not until Uncle Ulysses comes back anyway."

"Shucks, Homer, what can happen from playing a record?" Freddy demanded. "All that can happen is it can sound awful, or something like that, and we can be ready to put our hands over our ears, just in case."

Homer still looked doubtful, so Freddy said, "Grownups are always funny like that, anyway, Homer. You know that! They tell you not to listen to murders on the radio, and then give you a radio for Christmas. They tell you not to read comics, and they sell 'em like hotcakes. The sixth-grade teacher says, 'No gentleman chews bubble gum,' and her old man sells about a hundred sticks a day in his candy store. I don't see why you should be *afraid* to play —"

"I'm *not* afraid to play it!" Homer interrupted hotly, because his pride had been hurt. He jammed his hand into his pocket and jerked out his nickel. Then he marched straight up to the jukebox, poked one of the buttons, *the button,* the one without a name, and jammed his nickel into the slot.

There was a loud *cl-l-lick!* and mysteriously and silently the disgustingly unbreakable record slid out of the stack and began to spin. Both Homer and Freddy watched out of the corners of their eyes, wondering what kind of a weird noise, or music, or even a scream might come blaring out of the jukebox. They stood poised, hands ready to clap over their ears, prepared to dash out of the door.

As the music began flowing out of the jukebox, they sighed with relief and began to smile. It was only a gay little tune with a bouncing rhythm!

"That's sure a surprise!" said Homer, changing colors and nodding his head in time with the music.

"There's nothing wrong with that music!" said Freddy, beginning to tap his foot. "Golly, that's a catchy tune!"

After a few more measures of the catchy rhythm, a song began coming out of the jukebox:

"Sing hi-diddle-diddle,
For a silly little vittle.
Sing get-gat-gittle,
Got a hole in the middle.
Sing dough-de-dough-dough,
There's dough, you know.
There's not no nuts
In you-know-whats.
In a whole doughnut
There's a nice whole hole.
When you take a big bite,
Hold the whole hole tight.
If a little bit bitten,
Or a great bit bitten,
Any whole hole with a hole bitten in it,
Is a holey whole hole
And it JUST — PLAIN — ISN'T!"

After a few final measures of the catchy music, the record stopped playing. Freddy cried, "That's about the best tune I've ever heard, Homer, and the words are sort of good too. I'm gonna play that record *again!*"

Freddy deposited his nickel in the jukebox, and once more he and Homer nodded and tapped time to the tricky music and listened to the tricky words. Before the song was halfway through, they were singing gaily along with the voice coming from the jukebox:

"In a whole doughnut
There's a nice whole hole.
When you take a big bite,
Hold the whole hole tight.
  If a little bit bitten,
  Or a great bit bitten,
Any whole hole with a hole bitten in it,
Is a holey whole hole
And it JUST — PLAIN — ISN'T!"

"There just plain isn't anything wrong with that record," said Homer.

"Na-aw!" said Freddy. "The guy was nuts! Like you-know-whats!" Freddy giggled and hummed a few measures of the catchy tune.

"I could sit around," said Homer, "for a holey whole day and not do a thing but listen to it play."

"Say, Homer," said Freddy, starting to laugh, "do you-know-whats? You're talking, a little vittle bit funny!"

"Hawh!" Homer grinned at Freddy. "You're talking *notes*, just like *music*, and a little bit bitten funny too!"

"That's not nut-nothing," Freddy started to sing, "to get-gat-gittle excited about."

"No, not a bit bitten," Homer agreed.

"Not a little bit bitten," Freddy sang.

"Or a great bit bitten," Homer joined in.

"And any whole hole with a hole bitten in it, is a holey whole hole and it JUST PLAIN ISN'T!" They ended up singing as loud as they could sing and stamping time with their feet.

"That was just plain swell!" Freddy sang happily when they had finished.

"But, Freddy," Homer sang sadly, "we're a little bit bitten!"

"Or a great bit b —" Freddy stopped singing suddenly, and the smile faded slowly from his face. *"Holey whole holy smoke!"* he sang forte-forte.

"Yes, holey whole holy smoke," Homer encored in a pathetic piano-piano.

The barber put down the cards he had been dealing to Uncle Ulysses, Posty Pratt, and the mayor. He answered the telephone, listened for a minute, and then called over his shoulder, "Pipe down for a minute, you guys. Got a bad connection or something. Oh, Homer, it's you," he said, finally recognizing Homer's voice. "Yes, he's here. I'll call him to the phone." He jerked his thumb at Ulysses. "Homer is on the line. Says you better get-gat-gittle back to the lunchroom."

"Funny thing," the barber continued, "sounds just as though he were *singing!*"

"Hello, Homer," said Uncle Ulysses. "What? What? What's that you're singin'?" He listened attentively for a while and then asked anxiously, "But the *jukebox* stops playin' and singin', doesn't it? Oh, well," said Uncle Ulysses soothingly as he regained his smile, "that's nothing to worry a bit bitten about. For a minute I thought that the *jukebox* couldn't stop! Say, Homer, that's a good number you're singin'," Uncle Ulysses said. "Sing it just once more, please, from the beginning."

Uncle Ulysses, with the receiver pressed tight to his ear, stood swaying and tapping time with one foot, then with two feet, and then he started singing:

"In a whole doughnut
  There's a nice whole hole.
  When you take a big bite,
  Hold the whole hole tight.
    If a little bit bitten
    Or a great bit bitten,
  Any whole hole with a hole bitten in it,
  Is a holey whole hole
  And it JUST — PLAIN — ISN'T!"

"Thank you, Homer, that was just plain swell!"
Uncle Ulysses complimented with a cadenza. Then he
sang "Good-by!" and turned to the barber, the mayor,
and Posty Pratt, singing, "Drop your cards and get all
set, this song is swell for a male quartet!"

And it certainly was a swell song for a male quartet!
After about three practice tries, they rendered it in
perfect four-part harmony. They sang it a little bit
bitten better every time they sang it the holey whole
hole way through. By the time that Uncle Ulysses and

Posty Pratt discovered that they could not stop singing first and second tenor, and the mayor and the barber discovered that they could not stop singing alto and bass, they had already set a nonstop record for barbershop quarteting.

Finally four desperate men burst out of the barbershop, in the closest of close harmony, and went singing off in all directions.

When Uncle Ulysses came high-diddle-diddling through the door of the lunchroom he created a minor discord, until he started singing in the same key as Homer and Freddy and about two dozen or so after-the-movie customers. The customers, when they had first arrived in the lunchroom, had been very much taken by the charming little melody with the clever words that Homer and Freddy kept singing over and over again. One by one they too had joined in, and one by one they too had discovered that they could *not stop* singing the charming little melody with the clever words.

The soprano from the church choir was hitting A flat above high C and giving out with a get-gat-gittle that made every piece of glassware in the lunchroom vibrate and tingle. She was being well supported with dough-de-dough-dough from a full mixed chorus of male and female voices of all ages, not to mention all colors, thanks to the jukebox and its tastefully contrived lights.

Never, no never before had there been such a gay and carefree, downright enchanting song being sung by such a puzzled, downright unhappy gathering of people.

Homer was singing and singing, along with everybody else in the lunchroom. He was trying and trying, along with everybody else, to forget the clever words and the charming little melody. He tried singing another song, "Mary had a little vittle!" and couldn't get-gat-gittle past the very first line before he was right back dough-de-dough-doughing at the very top of his lungs.

He looked anxiously around him at the faces of some of the more experienced singers — the soprano, the deacon, the dentist, and Uncle Ulysses — all people who had been singing for years and years and could be more or less depended upon to sing in the proper key. They could always be depended upon to stop when they came to the end of the song, too. But not tonight! Tonight they couldn't even slow down, let alone stop!

"What if we *never* stop!" Homer began to worry.

"Somebody has to think of a cure," he thought, so he began to think just as hard as his poor young song-and-rhythm-racked mind could think. He remembered that something like this had happened to him once before. It was last September, when he had read a verse in a library book and couldn't stop repeating it. He remembered that there was a cure in the story. Now if he could only recall the name of that book, or the name of that story! Several times during the past hour he had been ever so close to remembering, but then suddenly he was caught up again in the catchy rhythm of the jukebox song.

Homer looked at the clock and saw that it was five minutes of nine. In five minutes the library would close for two weeks!

"We just got to find that book right away!" Homer thought. "We just got to get-gat-gittle that book from the library, no matter what!"

He waited for a moment, until the soprano finished off a particularly high and ear-piercing passage, then jumped up on the counter and soloed, "Every-body follow me-e-e, over to the librar-re-e-e!"

The soprano, having the loudest voice, spoke or rather sang for the entire group, "We will follow Homer Price, he can help us, ain't that nice?"

And they all danced out of the door after Homer,
singing:
        "... hi-diddle-diddle,
        For a silly little vittle.
        Sing get-gat-gittle,
        Got a hole in the middle.
        Sing dough-de-dough-dough,
        There's dough, you know.
        There's not no nuts
        In you-know-whats.

        In a whole doughnut
        There's a nice whole hole.
        When you take a big bite
        Hold the whole hole tight.
          If a little bit bitten,
          Or a great bit bitten,
        Any whole hole with a hole bitten in it,
        Is a holey whole hole
        And it JUST — PLAIN — ISN'T!"

It was closing time, and the librarian had just finished counting thirty-one pennies in fines from over-
due books. She glanced quickly around the library to
see if there was any last-minute thing to attend to

before she locked the door and went off on her vacation. She glanced thoughtfully down the neat shelves of books. Then she looked at the carefully stacked periodicals and made a quick mental note to renew the subscription to the *Musical Monthly* as soon as she returned. Then she closed the big dictionary that Freddy had left open, so dust would not settle on the page of "P's" during the next two weeks. At last everything was neat as a pin. Every chair and table was placed just so, and every last book was resting in its proper place, on its proper shelf.

"Now," she thought happily, "I can go on my vacation. *This* is the moment I have been waiting for!"

And *that* was the moment that Homer danced diddledy-viddledly in through the vestibule and *crash!* tripped over the standing sign that said QUIET, PLEASE.

The soprano hit high A flat right on the nose as she fell on top of him, followed by a mixed quartet, a trio, a couple of septets, a few odd stray singers, and Freddy, who had not had much previous musical experience.

Before this heap of melody had untangled itself completely, the mayor crescendoed into Uncle Ulysses' well-padded musical coda. Then the judge, a couple of city councilmen, and the dog warden sang in next, all dancing in an appropriate dignified manner.

Posty Pratt sang his way in at the head of his family of wife, daughters, sons-in-law, eight grandchildren, and an elderly second cousin of Mrs. Pratt's, who was having herself a high old time keeping time with her cane.

Homer wiggled to his feet and danced straight for the librarian. "We're a little bit bitten!" he sang. And the entire group chorused, "A little bit bitten, or a great bit bitten . . ." They sang the whole song for her, better than they had ever sung it. It really did sound wonderful, and it certainly showed what a little practice can accomplish.

The librarian could not help but be impressed with such beautiful singing, but after listening to three or four renditions she began to worry about catching her train and tried to ease people politely toward the door. When she began to have an irresistible urge to sing too, she began to understand the unhappy predicament of all of these forlorn souls who were singing such a gay and carefree little song.

"What can I do to help?" whimpered the librarian, trying her utmost not to sing the question.

"There's a book here on the shelves that'll tell us how to cure ourselves," Homer soloed.

"What's the title?" yelled the librarian, losing complete control of her library manner. "Do you know the author's name? What's the book's catalogue number?" she screamed.

"Dough-de-dough-dough, I do not know," sang Homer. "Those things I cannot remember, but I read it last September."

"Then there's nothing I can do, get-gat-gittle, I can't help you," the librarian chanted, beginning to be a wee bit bitten herself.

"We have to find a black-backed book, or maybe it's a brown-backed book," sang Homer. "And I think it was a little bit battered!"

Then everybody, the poor librarian included, joined in singing, "Find a black-backed book that's a little bit battered, or a brown-backed book that's a little bit battered." And at the same time everybody, the poor librarian included, started dancing past the shelves, snatching out every single brown-backed and black-backed book they came to.

"... dough-de-dough-dough,
There's dough, you know.
There's not no nuts
In you-know-whats!"

They all sang as they danced back and forth and in and out among the shelves of books. They started carrying an endless stream of brown-backed and black-backed books to where Homer was dancing and singing on the largest reading-room table. To most of these, which were the wrong shade of brown, or too thin, or too fat, or too battered, or too new, he just sang, "No!" or shook his head in time with the music. The books that Homer rejected were tossed in a disorderly heap that brought tears to the eyes and a sob to the contralto voice of the librarian.

Any books that looked about right as to size, color, or amount of battering, Homer quickly thumbed through, to see if he could find the story that he was sure would cure them of their terrible affliction.

"In a whole doughnut there's a nice whole hole," everybody was singing and singing, and then singing some more. The volume would gradually diminish as voices tired, and then someone's eye would light on a letter "O," or a number "800," and burst out with

a loud *"Holey whole hole!"* and that was enough to set everybody off at full blast again. They just couldn't stop singing the silly song. The more they sang, the more they danced past the shelves; the more they danced past the shelves, the more books they collected; and before very long Homer was perched in the middle of a tremendous pile of brown-backed and black-backed books that were a little bit battered, more or less.

There were books of art and biography, history and literature, philosophy, geography, geology, philology, zoology, and even economics, but Homer still hadn't found the book that he remembered reading last September. He courageously kept on looking, and everybody else kept on singing and dancing past the shelves, and bringing more and more books.

Freddy started dancing precariously along the balcony, and books started sailing over the railing to Homer, who caught them expertly to the tune of "High-diddle-diddle, for a silly little vittle," without skipping a single beat in the rhythm.

Suddenly the books that Freddy was lobbing from the balcony started sailing right on past Homer, because Homer was giving his undivided attention to a story in a slightly battered brown-backed book.

Almost before you could sing "Tom Robinson" everybody had gathered in a rhythmically swaying group around the base of the mountainous pile of books.

"Looky-look-look, it's a brown-backed book," sang the weary soprano.

"Get-gat-gittle, he's got a story in the middle," Uncle Ulysses sang hopefully in his tired tenor.

Suddenly Homer stopped swaying and bobbing. He smiled and kept reading, and then he started to sway and bob again. But while everybody else was swaying, Homer was bob-bobbing; and when the others bobbed, Homer swayed. Homer was caught by a *new* rhythm all his own. Then from the top of the pile of books he began to shout at the top of his voice.

> "Conductor, when you receive a fare,
> Punch in the presence of the passenjare!
> A blue-trip slip for an eight-cent fare,
> A buff-trip slip for a six-cent fare,
> A pink-trip slip for three-cent fare,
> Punch in the presence of the passenjare!
>
> CHORUS
>
> Punch, brothers, punch with care!
> Punch in the presence of the passenjare!"

Before Homer started shouting the second chorus of "Punch, brothers, punch with care!" the singers began to falter in their rhythm for the first time that evening. Then one by one they began to shout along with Homer, "A pink-trip slip for a three-cent fare," until everybody — yes, everybody — began to stamp his tired feet for joy and shout, "Punch, brothers, punch with care! Punch in the presence of the passenjare!"

That is, everybody except Homer. He sat smiling and out of breath on his perch atop the pile of books.

Everybody else was yelling, *"Punch, brothers, punch!"* and stamping so hard that the chandelier shook. The few red and blue and yellow books that remained on the shelves shook, even the QUIET PLEASE sign shook and rocked on its legs to the rhythm of the stamping. But not Homer. Homer was cured.

After he had rested for a moment and caught his breath, he slid unobserved down the pile of books.

"A blue-trip slip for an eight-cent fare!" Everybody was shouting and stamping so loud and so hard that Homer was completely ignored. He dodged expertly through the group without being stamped on, receiving only a light unintentional clip from the cane of Mrs. Pratt's elderly second cousin.

Homer needed somebody to help complete the cure

— anybody who had not yet heard the "Punch, brothers, punch" jingle. He rushed out of the door to bring back the very first person he should meet.

The chances were one hundred and two to one that it wouldn't be the person it was — there were at least one hundred and two Centerburg citizens who were not inside the library, but there she was, coming right up the library steps. It was the *sixth-grade teacher!*

"What has happened to Lucy?" she cried, referring to the librarian. "It's almost train time!"

"You've got to help," Homer said. "Come inside so they can tell you."

As they came in through the door, Homer shouted as he had never shouted before. "Tell it to her!" he bellowed, pointing to the sixth-grade teacher.

And they told her:

"Punch, brothers, punch with care!
Punch in the presence of the passenjare!"

They very generously told her two lines, all the way through, without holding back a single "Punch" or "Pink-trip slip."

Like all sixth-grade teachers, she was very quick to catch on — caught it good and perfect.

"A blue-trip slip for an eight-cent fare,
  A buff-trip slip for a six-cent fare,
  A pink-trip slip for a three-cent fare,
  Punch in the presence of the passenjare!"

Then, as suddenly as they had started shouting and stamping out the jingle, everybody stopped, just as Homer knew they would — everybody, that is, except the sixth-grade teacher. She'd caught it just too perfect, and she went right on shouting and stamping. Everybody else sat down, gasping for breath, right where they were, to rest their tired and aching feet.

Freddy, being young, recovered his wind quickly and edged his way over to where Homer stood.

"Now, what," he asked, nodding at the howling, stamping sixth-grade teacher, "are we going to do with *her?*"

"She'll be all right," Homer said confidently, "as soon as she tells it to somebody else. Just like I was cured when I told it to you, and you were cured when you told it to her."

"You mean to tell me that after you tell that jingle to somebody you forget it and are cured?" Freddy asked.

"Yep, that's the way it goes," said Homer, "just like in the book."

Freddy thought for a moment and then asked, "And the person she tells it to has to tell it to somebody else?"

"Yep, Freddy, somebody's *always* gonna be saying it," Homer admitted.

"Gets to be monotonous, doesn't it, Homer?" Freddy commented, shaking his head sadly toward the sixth-grade teacher, who was just beginning another chorus. "It will be terrible to have to listen to somebody around town keep on saying and saying that jingle forever and ever!"

"That will be better than having everybody in Centerburg keep on *singing* forever and ever," Homer argued. "And besides," he continued, "she's going on a vacation, isn't she? We'll just have to make sure that she gets on that train without telling somebody, and all our troubles will be over! C'mon, Freddy, we gotta get busy."

The two boys went around rousing everybody, making them put on their shoes, and explaining what had to be done about the poor teacher.

The mayor acted at once. While lacing his shoes, he appointed a committee of the two councilmen and the dog warden to collect baggage and to see the librarian and the teacher to the train.

Everybody filed out of the library. The librarian turned out the lights on the still swaying chandelier and locked the door on the shambles of her Dewey Decimal System. She helped lead the helplessly reciting teacher to a waiting car, and they were whisked away to catch the train.

"Golly, Uncle Ulysses," Homer said, suddenly remembering, "nobody has been looking after the lunchroom for a whole hour!"

"By jingo!" Uncle Ulysses snapped his fingers. "You'd better run right on back there, Homer! I've got a little matter to talk over with the barber and the mayor. Are you coming too, Posty?" he asked the postmaster.

Mrs. Pratt frowned, and Posty sheepishly said, "No," and marched away home at the head of his family.

Uncle Ulysses, the barber, and the mayor headed for the barbershop, and the soprano and all the others walked off on their tired and aching feet.

"We were awfully lucky, Homer, that somebody hadn't borrowed that book from the library," Freddy said as they settled down once more with their books. "We'd be singing yet!"

Homer nodded thoughtfully and didn't answer.

"What's the name of that book?" Freddy demanded.

"It's a book of stories by Mark Twain," Homer replied. "He's the same guy that wrote *Tom Sawyer* and *Life on the Mississippi,* and a lot of other good stories."

"It's sure a good book to know about," Freddy commented. "In case you ever need it again, you know just what to ask for. Say, Homer, how did that jingle go?"

"I can't remember, Freddy," Homer said. "That's the kind of jingle it is — you can't stop saying it until you tell it to somebody else, and then you forget all about it. I wish I'd thought to write the jingle down on a piece of paper and keep it handy. It's like you said, Freddy; a guy might need a jingle like that in a terrible hurry some time, and it could save an awful lot of trouble."

"I'll help you copy it, Homer," Freddy offered, "just as soon as the librarian gets back from Yellowstone Park."

"Why, hello, Sheriff," Homer greeted as the sheriff walked in the door. "Where have *you* been all evening?" he asked, remembering that the sheriff had not been a part of the strange singing and reciting.

"Over to the state capital," the sheriff said, nodding his greetings. "I was attending a meeting. I'm hungry, Homer. How about a cup of coffee and a piece of apple pie?"

"Sure thing, Sheriff," Homer said. "Freddy, you start some fresh coffee while I get the pie."

Both boys were hustling around behind the counter when they heard a *cl-l-lick!* that made their hair stand on end. When they turned, there was the sheriff, all grass green and smiling, standing next to the jukebox with his coin purse still in his hand.

"*What one are you playing?*" Freddy yelled, making a quick end run around the counter to look.

"It's — it's —" said Freddy in a terrified voice as he

watched the disgustingly unbreakable record slide out of the stack.

Then Freddy sighed with relief and changed to a brighter shade of lavender as the magic-like machinery quickly and silently flipped the record over.

"Golly, that was a close call!" cried Freddy. "For a moment I thought —"

Then a gay and lilting little melody began pouring out of the jukebox.

"That's nighty mice music," the sheriff said, beginning to nod in time with the melody.

And then the song began flowing out:

"A *hip*-high *hip*popotamus
Said, '*Hips* and lips make most of us.
From tip to tip a five-foot lip,
From *hip* to tip a three-foot foot.
With three-foot feet,
Our four feet meet
The ground, so we won't tip a bit.
I bet you never yet have met
A tippy, lippy, *hip*-high *hip*popotamus."

"Homer," Freddy gulped, "we got to get hold of that book — the one by the guy that wrote *Tom Sawyer* and *Life on the Mississ —*"

"Aht, aht, aht, aht!" Homer interrupted violently. "*Don't say Mississi* — the name of that river!"

Then he right away, fast as he could, filled two glasses with water. The two boys solemnly held their breath and counted to ten and drank the water down.

"There!" said Freddy, smiling once more, "that always cures my *hi* — makes them go away. I guess the whole thing was just our imaginations, eh, Homer?"

"Yeah, Freddy," said Homer, "we must have just dreamed the whole thing." Then, as the music coming from the jukebox ended with a spasmodic chord, Homer turned to the sheriff and said, "Sheriff, here's your piece of *hip* pie."